Look out for more **fabulous** picture books
by **Caryl Hart**.

KNOCK KNOCK
DINOSAUR

CARYL HART

NICK EAST

KNOCK KNOCK
PIRATE

CARYL HART & NICK EAST

For fun activities, further information and to order,
visit **www.hodderchildrens.co.uk**

For Jessie, Katinka & Andrew and all the
wonderful kids at Bakewell Junior School - C.H.

For the Pigs in Devon - S.H.

HODDER CHILDREN'S BOOKS
Originally published in 2010 as *Rhino What Rhino?*
This edition published in 2017

Text copyright © Caryl Hart, 2010
Illustrations copyright © Sarah Horne, 2010

A CIP catalogue record for this book is available from the British Library.

ISBN: 978 1 444 92520 3

1 3 5 7 9 10 8 6 4 2

Printed and bound in China

MIX
Paper from
responsible sources
FSC® C104740
www.fsc.org

Hodder Children's Books
An imprint of Hachette Children's Group
Part of Hodder and Stoughton
Carmelite House
50 Victoria Embankment
London EC4Y 0DZ

An Hachette UK Company
www.hachette.co.uk
www.hachettechildrens.co.uk

Hodder
Children's
Books

There once was a **rhino**

who lived at the zoo.

"I'm lonely," thought **Sidney**.

"There's **nothing to do!**"

So early one morning he SQUEEZED through the bars
and tiptoed away past the slumbering guards.

He **ran** till he reached a small farm by a lake.
Then came a great **rumble** that made the ground **shake.**

"It sounds like my tummy wants something to **eat**. Oh **look!** A plum pie. What a wonderful treat!"

"Who ate my lunch?"
Mr Potts shouted out.
And he turned to a **pig**
with a ring in his snout.

"My dinner has **vanished**.
My pudding's gone too.
No one else has come by
so it must have been **YOU!**"

"It's not ME!" oinked the pig as he nosed at the ground. "That **rhino** just took it while you weren't around."

Rhino? **What** Rhino?
That **cannot** be true.
There's only **one** rhino
and **he's** in the zoo.

Away **Sidney** strolled,
feeling **very** well fed.
"That pie was **delicious**
and so was that bread.

Now all I need is
an **outfit** to wear.
I'll just borrow a shirt
from that line over there."

"Look at my clothes!"
Aunt Ann cried in alarm.

And she glared at a **cow**
walking down to the farm.

"My tops are in **tatters**.
Those knickers were new.
No one else has come by
so it must have been **YOU!**"

"It's not ME!" mooed the cow with a flick of her ear.
"That **rhino** came creeping while you were not here."

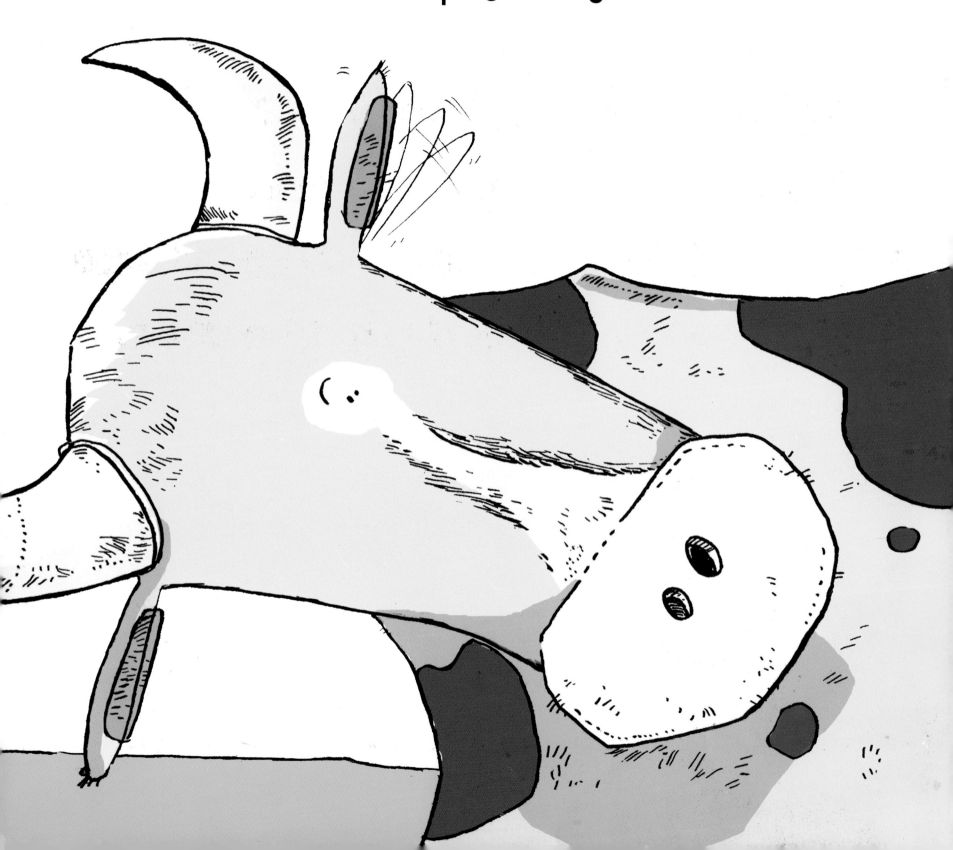

Rhino? **What** Rhino?
That **cannot** be true.
There's only **one** rhino
and **he's** in the zoo.

Aunt Ann searched the farmyard but **Sidney** had **gone**.
He felt **so** much smarter with proper clothes on.

"Now all I need is
a place for the night.
I'll sleep in this tree house,
I'm sure it's all right."

"Who wrecked my den?"
little Emily squealed.
And she spotted a **sheep**
trotting down through the field.

"My toys have been **trampled.**
That bike was brand new.

No one else has come by
so it must have been **YOU!**"

"It's not ME!" baaed the sheep, sitting down on a stool.
"That **rhino** crept up there while you were at school."

Rhino? **What** Rhino?
That **cannot** be true.
There's only **one** rhino
and **he's** in the zoo.

That evening while **Sidney** was curled up in bed, the animals met at the back of the shed.

"That **rhino** is causing such trouble," mooed cow. "Let's teach him a lesson. This has to stop **NOW**!"

"**Rhino**, now listen, it's time to **confess**.
You should be **ashamed**, making all this mess.
You've upset people and caused such a fuss.
They're all **hopping mad** and they're all blaming **us!**"

"You can't go on **helping yourself** all day long.
Stealing is **bad** – it's not fair and it's wrong.
You'll have to admit it. You know what to do.
Apologise now or go back to the zoo."

"**I beg** you," wailed Sidney,
"**Don't send me away!**

It's **no fun** being locked
in that cage every day.

I'll write them all letters
and say it was **me.**
I'll **stop** being greedy
and selfish – **you'll see.**"

Now **Sidney** works hard for his food and his bed.
He no longer **steals** lunches, but **cooks** them instead.

He says "**please**"
and "**thank you**"
and "how do you do?"

And he **NEVER, NO NEVER**

went back to the **zoo.**